Richard Egielski

SLIM
and
JIM

LAURA GERINGER BOOKS

An Imprint of HarperCollinsPublishers

Slim and Jim

Copyright © 2002 by Richard Egielski

Printed in Hong Kong All rights reserved.

www.harperchildrens.com

Library of Congress Cataloging-in-Publication Data

Egielski, Richard.

Slim and Jim / Richard Egielski

p.   cm.

Summary: Slim the rat and his new friend Jim the mouse find that their yo-yo tricks come in handy
when they are threatened by a tough, old, one-eyed cat.

ISBN 0-06-028352-1 — ISBN 0-06-028353-X (lib. bdg.)

[1. Rats—Fiction.   2. Mice—Fiction.   3. Cats—Fiction.   4. Yo-yos—Fiction.]   I. Title.

PZ7.E3215 Sp   2002   00-067281

[E]—dc21   CIP

                                                                                                                          AC

Typography by Alicia Mikles 1 2 3 4 5 6 7 8 9 10 ❖ First Edition

To my old pal, Sal Califano

Slious

Poor Slim. A young rat. Alone in the world. He lived as best he could. His only possession was an old yo-yo someone had given him a long time ago. "Maybe it was my mother," he thought.

One day Slim bumped into a tough, old, one-eyed cat named Buster.

"Hey, skinny!" Buster said. "I'll give you some food and a place to sleep if you'll do a job for me."

"Okay," said Slim.

Buster led Slim to his one-room dive. He gave him half a stale bialy to eat and a dirty sack to sleep on.

"Here's the plan, kid. There's this rich chicken, see, and she keeps her jewels in a box under her bed. She leaves her window open a crack. You're gonna squeeze through that crack, see? And hand me the box. Easy. Piece o' cake, right?"

"But that's stealing!" said Slim.

"Ha! Ha! Ha!" Buster laughed. "Who cares? Relax, kid. The job's tonight."

To pass the time, Slim did some yo-yo tricks: Johnny 'round the corner, walk the dog, rock the baby. Buster watched the yo-yo go up and down and up and down. He was mesmerized. You could have knocked him over with a feather.

That night, at the chicken's window, Slim froze. He wouldn't steal.

"Why, you worthless good-for-nothing!" Buster hissed. "I'll fix you!"

He smashed the window, grabbed the jewel box with one hand and Slim with the other, and raced across the rooftops.

"HELP!" screamed the chicken. "STOP, THIEF!"

Jim

Good Jim. A young mouse. He lived in a nice house with his dad, mom, and grandpa. Jolted awake by the noise, he jumped out of bed, threw on his bathrobe, darted up the roof to investigate . . .

and came face-to-face with Buster.

"STOP, THIEF!" Jim yelled.

"Who are you? Mighty Mouse?" Buster snarled. "Get out of my way!"

Jim tried to pull the jewel box away from Buster, but he lost his balance and they all tumbled off the roof. Buster landed in the back of a passing garbage truck as Slim and Jim plunged into the cold river.

Friends

Now, Slim, being a rat, was a good swimmer, but Jim, being a mouse, was not. With one small "Help!" Jim slipped beneath the surface. Slim dove down and pulled Jim back up. The strong current carried them far down the river until Slim caught hold of a pier and towed Jim to safety.

"Thanks," Jim gasped. "I didn't think you would save me. You're very nice for a thief."

"I'm no thief," Slim said, and he told Jim his sad life's story.

"Why not come home with me?" said Jim. "My parents won't mind—they love company."

"Gee, okay!" Slim answered. "I'm Slim."

"Pleased to meet you, Slim. I'm Jim."

Together they headed home. But walking through the dark, twisting streets of an unfamiliar part of town, they were soon lost. It began to rain. To warm himself up, Slim took out his yo-yo and did some tricks. He threw a sleeper, a breakaway, then a rock the baby.

"Wow! Not bad," said Jim. "Try this." And from his bathrobe
pocket he took out *his* yo-yo and did a rock the baby and throw it out
of its cradle. Slim countered with a rock the alien baby on the
launchpad. They threw tricks back and forth, laughing in the rain.

"Bravo!" cheered a big voice. "Stupendous!" cheered little voices.

It was a frog family returning home from a stroll in the rain.

Jim asked the big frog for directions back to his house.

"That's quite far," said the big frog. "It would take all night to walk there. You boys can stay here tonight, and I'll drive you home in the morning."

A New Home

When the car pulled up,
Jim's mom rushed out of the house.

"Oh, Jimmy! We were so worried.
Are you all right?"

"I'm fine, Mom," he replied, and told his family
what had happened.

Then he said, "Mom, Dad, Grandpa, this is my friend Slim. He saved my life. He has no family and no place to stay. Can he live with us?"

"But he's a rat!" said Grandpa. "Rats are nothing but trouble."

"Hush, Pop!" said Jim's dad. "He's Jim's friend. Of course he can stay."

The Birthday Present

From then on Slim and Jim were like brothers. Sharing the same room. Sharing yo-yo tricks. Slim finally had a real home.

One day Jim gave Slim a beautifully wrapped present. "Today is my birthday," he said. "But this is for you."

Slim unwrapped it. Inside was a brand-new yo-yo. It had a flashing light, and it whistled "Ob-La-Di, Ob-La-Da" as it whirled.

"Thanks," he whispered. "You're the best friend I've ever had."

That evening everyone gathered for Jim's birthday party. Even the
frog family was invited. Jim's mom brought out the cake. "Oh dear,
I forgot to buy candles."

Slim volunteered to run to the store. Jim's dad gave him the cash.

"I'll be back in a flash," said Slim as he ran out the door.

"Well, that's the last we'll see of him," said Grandpa. "You give a rat money, he won't come back. Just the way rats are."

"He will *so* come back!" Jim shouted. "Slim's my friend. You'll see."

It got later and later and Slim didn't come back. The cake sat untouched. Jim wouldn't let anyone have any until Slim returned. It grew dark, and the frog family went home. Jim's parents tried to comfort him. "You did your best to help Slim, honey. We're so sorry."

"I told you so," said Grandpa.

Kidnapped

Now, you and I know Jim was right and Slim intended to go back home. But just after he crossed the street, a paw reached out and pulled him into a dark alley.

"I said I'd fix you," a voice snarled. "Now you'll get it." Slim, scared stiff, couldn't utter a sound as Buster dragged him away.

That night Jim couldn't sleep. He got dressed and went for a walk. Wandering aimlessly, he soon found himself in a rough and shabby part of town. Just as he was about to head back home, he heard a tune. It was "Ob-La-Di, Ob-La-Da"! But where was it coming from? He looked up and saw a flashing light!

Jim climbed up the drainpipe and called, "Slim? Is that you?
Why did you leave us?"

Slim whimpered, "Jim! Help me! Buster kidnapped me!"

Jim began to shout as loud as he could, "HELP! POLICE! HELP!"

Lights flashed on. A crowd gathered. Sirens wailed. Buster
awoke. "What's going on? What's that racket?" he growled.

"Police—open up!"

Buster grabbed Slim by the collar and hauled him up the
ladder to the roof.

Jim followed close behind. "You leave Slim alone," he yelled.

"Well, if it isn't Mighty Mouse." Buster sneered. "I'll finish you once and for all."

He let go of Slim and bared his claws.

Seeing his friend in danger, Slim whipped out his yo-yo. A triple around-the-world super-loop combo. Buster froze. Jim joined in with a crazy cradle, a barrel roll, and a flying saucer. Slim threw a solar eclipse, a sidewinder, and a breakaway pinwheel. Buster's head jerked back and forth as the yo-yos flew. With a walk the dog on the kitty, Jim's yo-yo rolled over Buster's head, and down he went . . .

right into the arms of the police.

Dawn was breaking when Slim and Jim got home. Everyone was glad that Slim was back. Even Grandpa. "He's not so bad, for a rat," he grumbled.

Slim and Jim got even better with their yo-yo tricks. They began performing professionally.

When Buster was released from jail, Jim gave him a job in their show. One day Buster didn't show up for work, but he sent a note saying he was moving to France.

The boys continued on, traveling around the world with their yo-yo show. And to the end of their days, Slim and Jim remained the very best of friends.